D1191205

SWAMP CREATURE TEACHER

by John Sazaklis

illustrated by Patrycja Fabicka

PICTURE WINDOW BOOKS
a capstone imprint

Boo Books is published by
Picture Window Books, a Capstone imprint
A Capstone Imprint
1710 Roe Crest Drive
North Mankato, Minnesota 56003
www.capstonepub.com

Library of Congress Cataloging-in-Publication Data
Names: Sazaklis, John, author. | Fabicka, Patrycja, illustrator.
Title: Swamp creature teacher / by John Sazaklis ; illustrated by
Patrycja Fabicka.

Description: North Mankato : Picture Window Books, an imprint of
Capstone, [2021] | Series: Boo books | Audience: Ages 5-7. |

Summary: When a substitute teacher turns up in Joey and Johnny's
class, the boys quickly decide that she is a swamp creature, and after
school they set out to prove it; they follow her home to the swamp—but
Mrs. Gilman is not the only one living in the swamp, and if they are
not careful the boys may find themselves on the dinner menu.

Identifiers: LCCN 2019057128 (print) | LCCN 2019057129 (ebook) |
ISBN 9781515871101 (hardcover) | ISBN 9781515871156 (adobe pdf)

Subjects: LCSH: Substitute teachers—Juvenile fiction. | Monsters—
Juvenile fiction. | Swamps—Juvenile fiction. | Horror tales. | CYAC:
Substitute teachers—Fiction. | Monsters—Fiction. | Swamps—Fiction. |
Horror stories. | LCGFT: Horror fiction. | Humorous fiction.

Classification: LCC PZ7.D15134 Sw 2020 (print) | LCC PZ7.D15134
(ebook) | DDC 813.6 [E]—dc23
LC record available at https://lccn.loc.gov/2019057128
LC ebook record available at https://lccn.loc.gov/2019057129

Design Elements: Shutterstock: ALEXEY GRIGOREV, design element,
vavectors, design element, Zaie, design element

Designer: Sarah Bennett

Printed in the United States of America.
PA117

TABLE OF
CONTENTS

CHAPTER ONE

SOMETHING FISHY

It was a hot and humid day at Murky Meadows Elementary School. The kids in Mrs. Markela's class were waiting for their teacher. But she never showed up.

Suddenly, a tall, thin stranger entered. She had big bug eyes and puffy lips. She was dripping all over.

MRS. GILMAN

Drip. Drip. Drip.

"I am your substitute teacher, Mrs. Gilman," she said.

Two boys named Joey and Johnny were sitting in the back. Joey pointed to the puddle under Mrs. Gilman.

"Look how sweaty she is! She must be really nervous," whispered Joey.

"I don't think she's human," Johnny replied.

Joey's eyes went wide. "What do you mean?" he asked.

Johnny pulled out a comic book. "She looks just like this," he said. "And our school is next to a swamp. It makes sense."

"What's going on back there?" the teacher asked.

"Something fishy!" answered Johnny, holding up the book.

The students laughed.

Mrs. Gilman came face-to-face with Johnny.

"Not in my class," she hissed and snatched the book away.

CHAPTER TWO

SWAMPED

The morning dragged on. Johnny
spent it doodling in his notebook.
He was sure Mrs. Gilman was a
swamp creature. But how could
he prove it?

Finally it was time for lunch.

"Off with you, kids," Mrs. Gilman said. "I need to eat in peace."

Once she was alone, she dunked her head into the fish tank.

SPLASH!

Mrs. Gilman was enjoying her
lunch when someone knocked on
the door.

KNOCK! KNOCK!

She didn't hear anyone until it
was too late.

"What are you doing?" yelled
Johnny.

Mrs. Gilman pulled her head out
of the tank.

"Cooling off from the heat,"
replied Mrs. Gilman. "I'm feeling
a bit swamped!"

Then she cackled. Johnny saw
a mouth full of very sharp, very
pointy teeth.

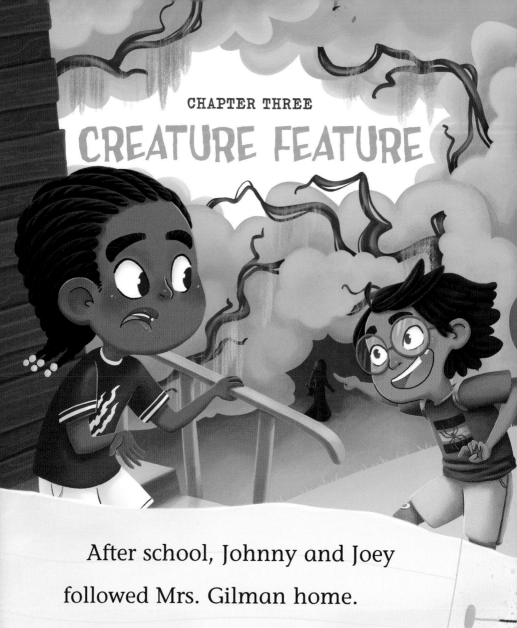

CHAPTER THREE
CREATURE FEATURE

After school, Johnny and Joey followed Mrs. Gilman home.

"Do you really think she's a swamp monster?" Joey asked.

"There's only one way to find out," said Johnny. "Let's go!"

The boys didn't have to go very far. Mrs. Gilman stopped at the swamp near the school. She quickly looked around. Then she walked right into it!

"I knew it!" Johnny cried. "Come on, Joey!"

The best friends crept closer to
the swamp. They did not see a large
figure coming up behind them.

"GOTCHA!" boomed a deep voice.

Towering over them was something
out of a comic book. Only it was real!

"Swamp creature!" the boys
screamed.

The monster lifted them high
and growled. "What are you doing
in my home?"

"Please don't eat us!" Joey cried.
"It was all his idea!"

"Hey!" Johnny shouted.

Just then Mrs. Gilman bubbled out of the swamp. "I see you've met some of my students, honey."

"Students?" asked the monster as he dropped the boys.

"Honey?" they replied wide-eyed.

"Yes, boys," said the teacher. "This is my husband."

The boys were speechless.

"The name's Finn. Pleased to meet you," the creature said.

He held out a webbed hand. It was slimy and wet. Johnny shook it. Joey did not.

Mrs. Gilman pulled out
Johnny's comic book.

"Hey! That's Finn on the cover!"
Johnny exclaimed.

"I thought I would surprise
you and get it autographed,"
Mrs. Gilman said.

She gave it to Finn.
He stamped it with his
webbed hand, leaving
a slimy handprint.

"I can't believe they're real swamp creatures," Joey whispered.

"I told you so," Johnny replied. "And you are holding the proof!"

"Would you like to stay for dinner?" asked Mrs. Gilman.

"Sure," said Joey. "What are you having?"

The swamp creatures flashed their pointy teeth and shouted, "YOU!"

"Help! Swamp creatures!" the boys
hollered as they ran away.

Finn picked up the comic book
that Johnny had dropped and took
a bite out of it.

"That never gets old," he said.

"Do you think anyone will believe
them?" asked Mrs. Gilman.

"They never do," said Finn.

The swamp creatures laughed and dove into their underwater home for a relaxing night.

AUTHOR

John Sazaklis is a *New York Times* bestselling author with almost 100 children's books under his utility belt! He has also illustrated Spider-Man books, created toys for *MAD* magazine, and written for the BEN 10 animated series. John lives in New York City with his superpowered wife and daughter.

ILLUSTRATOR

Patrycja Fabicka is an illustrator with a love for magic, nature, soft colors, and storytelling. Creating cute and colorful illustrations is something that warms her heart—even during cold winter nights. She hopes that her artwork will inspire children, as she was once inspired by *The Snow Queen*, *Cinderella*, and other fairy tales.

GLOSSARY

cackle (KAK-uhl)—to laugh in a sharp, loud way

doodle (DOO-duhl)—to draw without thinking

hiss (HISS)—to make a noise like a snake

humid (HYOO-mid)—damp or moist

substitute (SUHB-stuh-toot)—something or someone used in place of another

swamped (SWAHMPT)—having way too much to do

webbed (WEBBED)—having folded skin or tissue between an animal's toes or fingers

DISCUSSION QUESTIONS

1. Were you surprised that the teacher really was a swamp monster? Why or why not?

2. Do you think it was a good idea for the boys to follow Mrs. Gilman? Would you have done the same thing?

3. What do you think would have happened if the boys had stayed for supper?

WRITING PROMPTS

1. Write a few sentences about your favorite substitute teacher.

2. Draw a picture of your own swamp monster. Then write a few sentences describing your monster. Be sure to give it a name.

3. The author includes clues in the story before he tells you that the teacher is a swamp monster. One is her name. Make a list of at least three other clues the author uses.

SCARED SILLY JOKES!

What is a swamp monster's favorite treat?

marsh-mallows

What do you call a fish in a suit?

so-FISH-ticated

How do fish always know how much they weigh?

They have their own scales.

What kind of fish chase mice?

catfish

What do fish need to stay healthy?

vitamin sea

What is the most valuable type of fish?

a goldfish

Why did the fish go to Hollywood?

She wanted to be a starfish.

If fish lived on land, which country would they live in?

Finland

BOO BOOKS

Discover more just-right frights!

CLOWNS FROM OUTER SPACE

GAME OVER

SLIME TIME!

SWAMP CREATURE TEACHER

ATTACK OF THE CUTE

CAMPFIRE VAMPIRE

THE HAUNTED BACKPACK

NIGHT OF THE DIGGING DOG

SCARE BALL

WITCH'S STEW

Only from Capstone